DISCARD

BO

Cinco de Mayo

by Janet Riehecky
illustrated by Krystyna Stasiak

created by Wing Park Publishers

CHILDRENS PRESS®
CHICAGO

Sincere appreciation is expressed to the Elgin Hispanic Fine Arts Council for providing background information for this book.

Library of Congress Cataloging-in-Publication Data

Riehecky, Janet, 1935-
   Cinco de Mayo / by Janet Riehecky ; illustrated by Krystyna Stasiak
      p.   cm. — (Circle the year with holidays)
   "Created by Wing Park Publishers."
   Summary: Although Maria is not too successful at helping her family prepare for Cinco de Mayo, she wins an art contest at the library and gets to break the pinata back home. Includes instructions for making tacos and crafts.
   ISBN 0-516-00681-9
   [1. Cinco de Mayo (Mexican holiday)—Fiction.]
I. Stasiak, Krystyna, ill.   II. Title.   III. Series.
PZ7.R4277Ci   1993
[E]—dc20
                                          93-13249
                                            CIP
                                            AC

Maria woke up early. When she remem-
bered it was Cinco de Mayo, a fiesta day, she
jumped quickly out of bed. "What a fun day
this will be," she said.

Already her Mom was cooking. Maria could smell the tacos, tostados, enchiladas, and other special dishes. She hurried to the kitchen doorway and stood watching.

"It smells great!" Maria said. "Mom, can I help?"

Mrs. Sanchez smiled. "All right," she said.
"You can grate the cheese."

Maria picked up the big block of cheese
and scraped it across the grater. The cheese
slipped from her hands. "Oh, no," cried Maria
as she knocked over the bowl.

Mrs. Sanchez began cleaning up the mess.
"Maria," she said. "The cheese block is too
big for your hands. Why don't you find
something else to do?"

Maria hung her head and walked slowly out
of the kitchen. Soon she heard the noise of
a hammer in the front yard.

Maria peeked out and saw her father. He
was decorating the front yard with straw
animals. "Dad," she called. "It looks great!"
The animals did look very special. There was

a donkey, a cat, a bear, and a monkey. Maria's
father and brother, Ramon, had made them.
They had twisted the shapes from straw and
painted them in bright colors.

9

Mr. Sanchez was pounding a stake into the
ground to hold the monkey.

"Can I help?" Maria asked.

"Sure," said her father. "Would you like to
swing the hammer?"

Maria smiled and hurried down the steps.
She picked up the hammer and swung with
all her might. The hammer came down, missing
the stake and striking her father's thumb.

"Yow," yelled Mr. Sanchez. He took the
hammer from Maria. "Maybe this wasn't such
a good idea," he said, "for such a little girl?
Why don't you go find something else to do?"

Maria left, hanging her head. As she walked
away, she could hear music coming from the
garage. Her brother, Ramon, and five of his
friends were practicing. They had a mariachi
band.

"You guys sound great," she said. "May I play?" She reached out and plucked a string on Ramon's guitar. It made a loud, moaning sound as it broke.

"I'm sorry, Maria," said Ramon. "We're
playing for the festival this afternoon. We don't
have time to play with you."

Maria walked slowly back into the house.
There her sister, Anna Louisa, was decorating.
Anna Louisa had put paper flowers on the table
and in the window. There were streamers of
red, white, and green hanging from the ceiling.
Anna Louisa was standing on a chair adding
paper lanterns.

"It looks great!" said Maria. "May I help?"

Anna Louisa smiled. "Would you hand me another lantern?" she asked.

Maria grabbed a paper lantern from the box. As she pulled it out, it ripped in two. She began to cry.

Anna Louisa jumped down and pulled Maria into her arms. "It's all right, Maria," she said. "We have lots more lanterns."

"Every time I try to help, I break something," Maria cried.

Anna Louisa thought for a minute. "I know what you could do," she said. "Why don't you draw a picture for the contest at the library? Children from all over the city are drawing pictures to celebrate Cinco de Mayo."

Maria got out her crayons and a big piece of paper. She thought about everything her family was doing to celebrate. She divided the paper into four sections. Then she drew a picture of her mother cooking, her father setting up the straw animals, her brother playing in the band, and her sister putting up the decorations. "Fiestas are fun," she said.

When she was done, she showed the picture
to Anna Louisa. Anna Louisa smiled. "I'll take
you to the library so we can enter it in the
contest," she said. And she did.

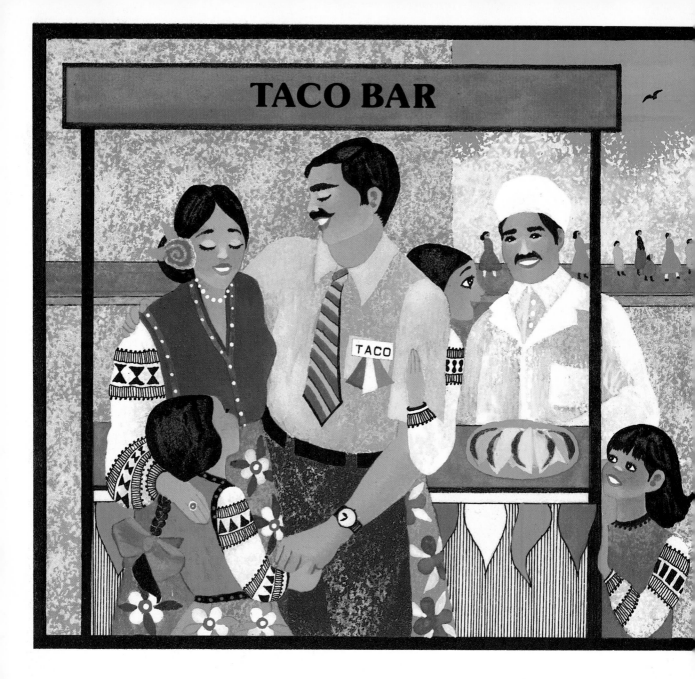

Later that day, the entire Sanchez family went to the city plaza to celebrate. First they visited brightly-colored booths where snacks and different craft items were sold. In one booth there was a taco-eating contest. Mr. Sanchez entered and won!

At the end of the plaza, dancers dressed in beautiful costumes performed, while Ramon's mariachi band played lively music. Everyone laughed and cheered!

"Let's go over to the library and check out
the contest," Anna Louisa said.

When the family entered the lobby, they saw

lots of pictures. But right in front with a big blue ribbon was Maria's picture.

"Oh, Maria," everyone exclaimed. "You won! You won!" Maria felt proud and happy.

In the evening, the family went back to the house to enjoy all the special fiesta food. Aunt Juanita and Uncle Benito and their children came over too.

After dinner, Uncle Benito told the children the story of Cinco de Mayo—how the Mexicans years before had defeated the French in battle. Everyone cheered!

Then Uncle Benito brought out the piñata he had made for the children. Each child took a turn being blindfolded and swinging at the piñata. When it was Maria's turn, she swung with all her might. CRACK! The piñata burst, spilling candy everywhere!

"I knew my talent for breaking things would
come in handy," she said with a laugh, as she
and her cousins gathered up the candy. "But
this time I was supposed to break something!"

It had been a great fiesta! "Happy Cinco de
Mayo," they all said to one another.

29

ACTIVITIES

Teachers will need to help.

Paper Flowers

Paper flowers are traditional decorations for Cinco de Mayo. Here's one easy pattern to make.

You will need: colored tissue paper, paper fasteners, wire, florist tape, scissors.

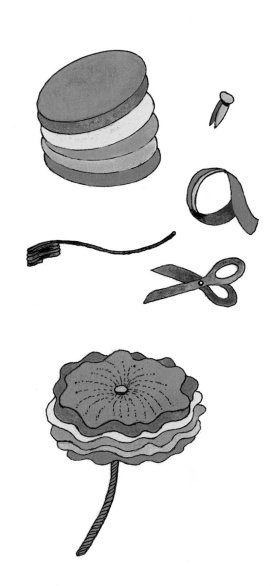

1. Cut circles from tissue paper about six inches in diameter.

2. Stack five or six circles of tissue paper and fasten in the center with a paper fastener.

3. Do not spread apart the paper fastener at the bottom. Instead use the florist tape to attach a piece of wire to the paper fastener.

4. Wrap the entire wire for the stem.

5. Then, taking each piece of tissue paper separately, lift and crinkle the tissue paper to form the flower.

Paper Lanterns

You can buy paper lanterns in a store, but it's more fun to make them.

You will need: 11" x 17" construction paper of various colors, scissors, glue or tape, hole punch, string.

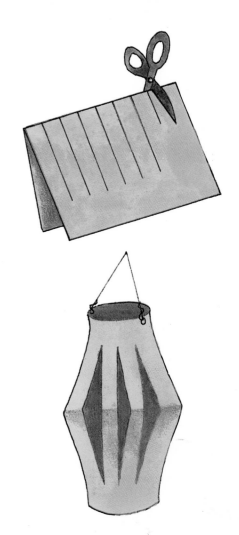

Fold construction paper in half forming an 11" x 8½" rectangle. Working on the fold edge, make cuts in the paper. Starting 1" from the corner, make a 5½" deep cut in the paper. Make a parallel cut each inch across the paper. Unfold and then use tape or glue to fasten together the paper edges so that the lantern is 17" tall and the cuts run up and down. Use the hole punch to punch two holes on opposite sides of the top. Put string through the holes and hang your paper lantern anywhere!

Tacos

Tacos are a fun Mexican dish, so why not have a taco bar to celebrate Cinco de Mayo?

You will need: taco shells, prepared taco sauce, hamburger, cheddar cheese, onions, green peppers, tomatoes, lettuce, green olives, black olives, and anything else you like on a taco; small dishes and serving spoons.

Brown hamburger and break it into small pieces. Grate cheese. Slice or dice everything else and put each item into its own small bowl with a serving spoon. Children can help prepare the food if properly supervised. Your guests can take a taco shell, add hamburger, sauce, and whatever ingredients they like.

CINCO DE MAYO

Cinco de Mayo is a holiday celebrated in Mexico and by people of Mexican descent to remember a famous battle fought May 5, 1862. In 1862, Mexico had just set up a republican form of government and elected their first president. Many people in Europe didn't like this. They thought that the Mexicans wouldn't be able to govern themselves. And they also thought that Mexico had unlimited amounts of gold, which they wanted for themselves. France used the fact that Mexico owed them money as an excuse to invade Mexico.

France sent its best-trained and best-equipped troops to Mexico, under the command of a famous general. They thought it would be easy to defeat the Mexicans, who had little equipment and little training. Their first attack was against a fort in the town of Puebla. The Mexican army of only three hundred soldiers was joined by three thousand Mexican Indians. Most were armed only with sticks and stones, but three times the French charged and three times the Mexicans beat them back. Finally the French had to give up.

Mexicans are very proud that they fought for freedom and that they were able to beat the powerful French invaders. And every year they remember the battle in which they did that when they celebrate Cinco de Mayo.